Milly and Molly

Part of the proceeds from the sale of this book goes to The Friends of Milly, Molly Inc., a charity which aims to promote the acceptance of diversity and the learning of life skills through literacy – *"for every child, a book"*.

Milly, Molly and I Love You

Published by
MM House Publishing
P O Box 539
Gisborne, New Zealand
email: books@millymolly.com

ISBN: 1-86972-047-4

10 9 8 7 6 5 4 3 2 1

Milly, Molly
and
I Love You

"We may look different
but we feel the same."

On December the fifth, Goldie died of old age.
"You have looked after her beautifully,"
comforted Miss Blythe.

“But did you ever tell Goldie you loved her?”
Milly and Molly shook their heads.

“I think we need to say, I love you, more often,” Miss Blythe said softly. “Everyone loves to hear it.”

Milly and Molly nodded.

Miss Blythe took care of Goldie and gave Milly and Molly a hug.
"We love you Miss Blythe," they said.
"I love you too," Miss Blythe said warmly.

On the way home, Milly and Molly bumped into Farmer Hegarty walking Pennyroyal to the vet.

"We love you Farmer Hegarty," they called.

Farmer Hegarty smiled from ear to ear.
"You've made my day," he said.
"I love you too."

Milly and Molly passed Aunt Maude in her vegetable garden.
"We love you Aunt Maude," they said.

“Good heavens,” said Aunt Maude with a start. “I love you too.”

BushBob came around the corner with his parrot. “We love you BushBob,” called Milly and Molly.

“Well aren’t I the lucky one,” said BushBob with a smile. “I love you too.”

Milly and Molly met Doctor Smiley bustling along with his black bag. “We love you Doctor Smiley,” they said.

Doctor Smiley stopped short with a little cough and a smile. "I love you too," he said.

Milly and Molly found Maxter's mother standing at the end of her driveway looking anxious. "We love you," they called.

“Well, well, well,” said Maxter’s mother slowly. “I love you too.”

And then along came Father Brownlie.
"We love you Father Brownlie," said Milly and Molly.

“Bless you both,” said Father Brownlie with a bigger smile than usual. “I love you too.”

Old Frosty was raking leaves in his garden.
"We love you," called Milly and Molly.

“That’s the nicest thing I’ve ever heard,” said Old Frosty with a blush. “I love you too.”

Milly and Molly found Mr. Limpy collecting his paper.
"We love you Mr. Limpy," they said.

"My little rays of sunshine," Mr. Limpy said warmly. "I love you too."

And then Milly and Molly saw Marmalade and Tom Cat waiting for them at the gate.

“We love you Marmalade and Tom Cat,”
they said as they swooped them up.

Marmalade and Tom Cat had heard it all a million times before. They just closed their eyes and purred.

PARENT GUIDE

Milly, Molly and I Love You

The value implicitly expressed in this story is 'love' - to like someone or something with all your heart.

Milly and Molly learn how delighted their friends are to hear the words 'I love you'.
Marmalade and Tom Cat, who have heard the words a million times before, are happy, contented friends and give love and affection in return.

"We may look different but we feel the same."

Other picture books in the Milly, Molly series include:

- Milly, Molly and Jimmy's Seeds ISBN 1-86972-000-8
- Milly, Molly and Beefy ISBN 1-86972-006-7
- Milly, Molly and Pet Day ISBN 1-86972-004-0
- Milly, Molly and Oink ISBN 1-86972-002-4
- Milly and Molly Go Camping ISBN 1-86972-003-2
- Milly, Molly and Betelgeuse ISBN 1-86972-005-9
- Milly, Molly and Taffy Bogle ISBN 1-86972-001-6
- Milly, Molly and Alf ISBN 1-86972-018-0
- Milly, Molly and Sock Heaven ISBN 1-86972-015-6
- Milly, Molly and the Sunhat ISBN 1-86972-016-4
- Milly, Molly and Special Friends ISBN 1-86972-017-2
- Milly, Molly and Different Dads ISBN 1-86972-019-9
- Milly, Molly and Aunt Maude ISBN 1-86972-014-8
- Milly, Molly and Henry ISBN 1-86972-030-X
- Milly, Molly and the Secret Scarves ISBN 1-86972-027-X
- Milly, Molly and the Stowaways ISBN 1-86972-026-1
- Milly, Molly and the Tree Hut ISBN 1-86972-028-8
- Milly, Molly and What Was That ISBN 1-86972-031-8
- Milly, Molly and Grandpa Friday ISBN 1-86972-029-6
- Milly, Molly and Beaky ISBN 1-86972-048-2
- Milly, Molly and the Bike Ride ISBN 1-86972-046-6
- Milly, Molly and the Ferryman ISBN 1-86972-044-X
- Milly, Molly and the Picnic ISBN 1-86972-045-8
- Milly, Molly and the Runaway Bean ISBN 1-86972-049-0